Stop Those Painters!

by Rita Golden Gelman

Pictures by Mort Gerberg

SCHOLASTIC INC.

New York   Toronto   London   Auckland   Sydney

For the García family of Managua,
with love and thanks. Especially the kids:
Sly, Cristian, Fabiola, Gabriela,
Sofo Nias, Mario, Alejandra, Chele,
Alvaro, Juan Carlos, Yesica, Ana
—R.G.G.

For Stephanie and Michael
—M.G.

ISBN 0-590-40959-X

Text copyright © 1989 by Rita Golden Gelman.
Illustrations copyright © 1989 by Mort Gerberg.
All rights reserved. Published by Scholastic Inc.
HELLO READER is a trademark of Scholastic Inc.
Art Direction by Diana Hrisinko.
Text Design by Theresa Fitzgerald.

12 11 10 9 8 7 6 5 4 3 2 1   9/8 0 1 2 3 4/9

Printed in the U.S.A.
First Scholastic printing, April 1989

Painters.

Painters painting.

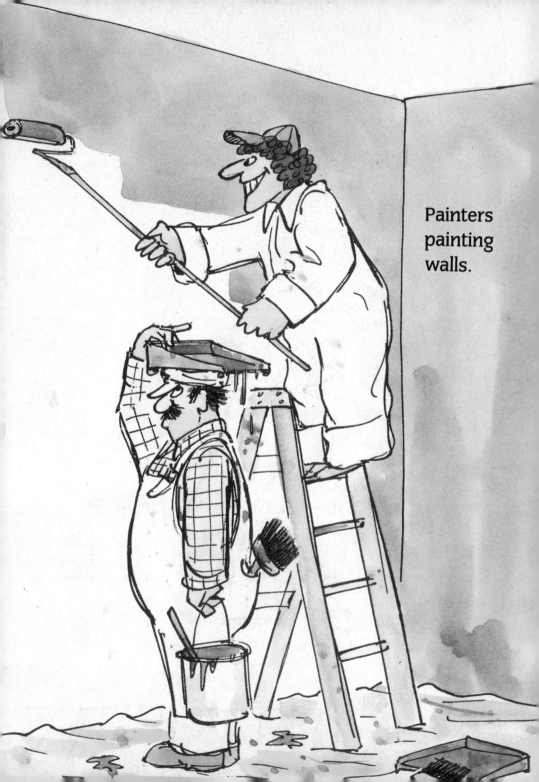

Painters
painting
walls.

Painters painting halls.

Painters painting windows?

No!
Stop those painters.
Make them go!

Painters painting stairs.

Painters painting chairs.

Painters painting ham and cheese.

Don't paint my bike.
Don't paint my bat.

Painters, no!
You can't paint that!

Painters painting grass and trees.

Painters painting birds and bees.

Stop those painters.
Please! Please! Please!

Oh, no!
A mouse.
A dog.
A cow!

Stop those painters.
Stop them now!

Painted teachers.
Painted toys.

Painted girls.
Painted boys.

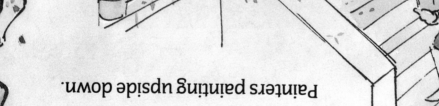

Painters painting upside down.

Get those painters out of town!

Painters painting cars and trains.

Painters painting trucks and planes.

Look! A jet with people in it.

Stop, you painters!
Stop this minute.

There they go!
They're gone.

Good-bye!

Oh, look—

A rainbow in the sky.